For Tamara, Ashley, and Jody, with love —V. B.
To Cherry and Sophie —D. A.

Glossary

A **guinep** is a small fruit that can be popped into your mouth once you have cracked open the outer shell.

A **jackfruit** is a large oval fruit. Inside the spiky green skin there are cream-colored, chewy pods, each containing a cream-colored seed.

A **june-plum** is a delicious yellow fruit with a large pit.

A **pawpaw** is a papaya, an oblong, yellowish, tasty fruit with many seeds.

A **naseberry** (also called sapodilla) is a brown fruit with rough skin and sweet pulp.

The **red apples** in the text are Caribbean Otaheiti apples. They are pear shaped and very sweet and juicy.

Smaddy means "somebody."

A **sweet-sop** is a very sweet fruit that has a rough outside and a white inside with black seeds.

Throughout the text, the spelling reflects the sound of the Jamaican language, Patwa. However, for the sake of clarity, some words were not changed. (For example, "can't" was not changed to "cyan.")

Henry Holt and Company, Inc.
Publishers since 1866
115 West 18th Street
New York, New York 10011

Henry Holt is a registered trademark of Henry Holt and Company, Inc.
"Fruits" is taken from *Duppy Jamboree,*
first published by Cambridge University Press in 1992.
Text copyright ©1992 by Valerie Bloom.
Illustrations copyright ©1996 by David Axtell. All rights reserved.
First published in the United States in 1997 by Henry Holt and Company, Inc.
Published in Canada by Fitzhenry and Whiteside Ltd.,
195 Allstate Parkway, Markam, Ontario L3R 4T8.
Originally published in the United Kingdom in 1996 by
Macmillan Children's Books, a division of
Macmillan Publishers Limited, London.

Library of Congress Cataloging-in-Publication Data
Bloom, Valerie.
Fruits: a Caribbean counting poem / by Valerie Bloom; illustrated by David Axtell.
Summary: This poem counts up to ten different kinds of Caribbean fruit, including guavas, jack-fruit, and Otaheiti apples.
1. Caribbean Area—Juvenile poetry. 2. Children's poetry, Jamaican. 3. Counting-out rhymes.
[1. Caribbean Area—Poetry. 2. Counting. 3. Fruit—Poetry. 4. Caribbean poetry (English)]
I. Axtell, David, ill. II. Title. PR9265.9.B58F78 1996 811—dc20 96-28890

ISBN 0-8050-5171-6
First American Edition—1997
Printed and bound in Great Britain by
BPC Consumer Books Ltd
A member of
The British Printing Company Ltd

FRUITS

A Caribbean Counting Poem

by Valerie Bloom

illustrated by David Axtell

Henry Holt and Company • New York

Half a pawpaw in de basket—
Only one o' we can have it.
Wonder which one dat will be?
Ah have a feelin' dat is me.

One guinep up in de tree
Hangin' down dere tempting me.
It don' mek no sense to pick it,
One guinep can't feed a cricket.

Two ripe guava 'pon de shelf,
Ah know ah hide dem dere meself.
When night come an' it get dark
Me an' dem will have a talk.

Tree sweet-sop, well ah jus' might
Give one o' dem a nice big bite.
Cover up the bite jus' so, Sis,
Den no one will ever notice.

Four red apple near me chair—
Who so careless put dem dere?
Dem don' know how me love apple?
Well, tank God fe silly people.

Five june-plum, ah can't believe it!
How dem know june-plum's me fav'rit?
But why dem hide dem in de cupboard?
Cho, people can be so awkward.

Six naseberry, you want a nibble?
Why baby must always dribble?
Come wipe you mout', it don' mek sense
To broadcast de evidence.

Seven mango! What a find!
De smaddy who lef dem really kind.
One fe you an' six fe me,
If you want more, climb de tree.

Eight orange fe cousin Clem,
But ah have just one problem—
How to get rid o' de eight skin
Dat de orange, dem come in.

Nine jackfruit! Not even me
Can finish nine, but let me see,
Ah don' suppose dat dem will miss one.
Dat was hard, but now me done.

Ten banana, mek dem stay,
Ah feelin' really full today.

Mek me lie down on me bed, quick.
Lawd, ah feelin' really sick.

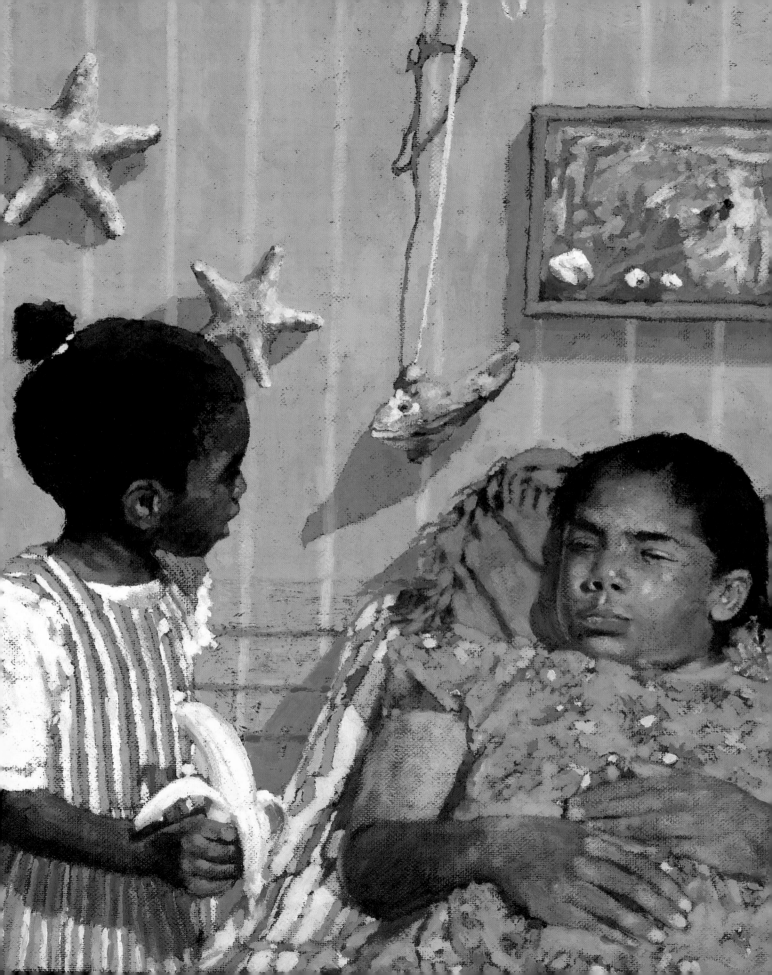